ISBN 0–85079–187–1

RUPERT

THE DAILY EXPRESS ANNUAL

John Harrold

No 54

Published by Express Newspapers p.l.c., Blackfriars Road, SE1 9UX

£3·85

RUPERT

Rupert and Bill run free as air
Till something makes them stop and stare.

"Hey, Rupert! Look at that!" Rupert's pal Bill Badger breaks off from the race the pair are having high on Nutwood Common and points. Sticking out of a nearby tree stump is an arrow. But it's no ordinary arrow, as the pals discover when they get close. It is made of shiny metal, it's big and it is making a humming sound. As long as it's buzzing neither of them feels like touching it.

This Book Belongs To:

....

CONTENTS

WRITTEN AND EDITED BY JAMES HENDERSON
ILLUSTRATED BY JOHN HARROLD
STORY COLOURING BY DORIS CAMPBELL

and the **Boomerarrow**

A gleaming arrow's what they've found
Which makes a curious humming sound.

Although it's stuck fast in a tree,
Together they can pull it free.

Then suddenly the sound stops. The pals wait a little then Rupert says, "Shall we try to get it out of the stump?" Bill nods. So Rupert has a go at freeing it. It won't budge. Bill tries. Just the same. Then Rupert grasps it, Bill holds him round the waist, they tug – and out it comes. "I say, it's a beauty!" breathes Rupert. "I wonder how it got here and whose arrow it can be."

"A beauty!" both the friends agree,
"But whose," asks Rupert, "can it be?"

RUPERT TRIES OUT THE ARROW

Before surrendering his find
Rupert first has some fun in mind.

"Let's fire the arrow from my bow,
I wonder how far it will go?"

Bingo's amused by this new sport
But scoffs as both their shots fall short.

"The bow's too small, that's what's amiss,
You'll need a stronger one for this!"

Well, plainly the arrow belongs to someone so, of course, Rupert and Bill decide the right thing to do is hand it in to PC Growler, Nutwood's village bobby. "But there can't be any harm in our having a go with it first," Rupert grins. So back the pair go to Rupert's cottage where Rupert fetches out his small toy bow. It makes the arrow seem even bigger. He is fitting it to the bow when another of his pals, Bingo the clever pup, turns up.

Neither of the others notices him until he gives a snort of laughter at Rupert's attempt to fire the big arrow. "You'll never fire it with that teeny bow!" he scoffs. "Here, let me try," says Bill. "I'll show you!" But his effort is no better and Bingo laughs even louder. "If you're so clever . . ." Rupert begins. "Oh, I am," chuckles Bingo. "But not with a toy bow. Come to my house and I'll show you." So off the three troop.

RUPERT'S PAL WANTS TO TRY IT

Their chum has something they must see,
He's interested in archery.

"I'm not the only one!" he adds,
"It's one of the Professor's fads."

And now with pride the clever pup
Reveals a gadget he's thought up.

"Before we fire this bow of mine,
We'll tie the arrow to some twine."

Everyone in Nutwood thinks of Bingo as "the clever pup" because he is forever inventing and making things. Not all work, but quite a lot do. On the way to his place he confides, "This arrow's just what I've been looking for." "Oh, you mustn't keep it!" protests Rupert. "We were going to take it to PC Growler when we'd tried it out. He'll find out whose it is." "I'm pretty sure whose it is," smiles Bingo as they reach his workshop. "The Professor's!"

The Professor is a clever old man who lives with a servant in a tower near the village. "He and I are competing to see who can make a machine to launch an arrow the farthest," says Bingo as he throws open the door. "Here's mine! My electric crossbow! I haven't made an arrow yet so we'll try it out with the Professor's. And just to make sure we don't lose it as he seems to have done . . ." He reaches down from a shelf a long coil of stout twine.

RUPERT HELPS WITH THE TEST

"This arrow's too sharp!" Rupert calls,
"It might hurt someone when it falls."

Such problems don't stump Bingo though.
He's got the answer, you might know!

"An old sink plunger!" Rupert cries,
"A perfect fit!" the pup replies.

While Bill helps Rupert tie a knot,
Bingo prepares to fire the shot.

As Rupert and Bill help him to move his machine outside, Bingo explains that one end of the twine will be tied to the arrow, the other to something firm here. "But we can't just fire it anywhere," Rupert points out. "It's too sharp. It might hurt someone." "You're right!" says Bingo and disappears indoors to reappear with the sort of rubber plunger you use for unstopping blocked sinks. "Now what's he up to?" gasps Bill.

"An old sink plunger!" Rupert exclaims. "What for?" Bingo's answer is to remove the plunger's handle and fit the rubber part over the arrow's point. "A perfect fit!" he grins. "Just like those toy sucker ones that stick to the target." Now, while Rupert ties the twine to the arrow, Bingo gets the machine ready. A battery motor draws back the bowstring. He pulls a knob. "This holds the bowstring in position," he says. "I just move it back to fire the arrow."

RUPERT FINDS HIMSELF FLYING

"The crossbow's ready, looking fine!
Here, Rupert! Just secure the line!"

Then Bingo turns and cries, "Oh no!"
He's accidentally fired the bow . . .

Not ready for this sudden flight,
Poor Rupert gets an awful fright.

Too late to let go, he's so high,
He's yanked at top speed through the sky.

The electric crossbow is ready. The bowstring is drawn back and locked in position by one of the knobs. Bingo fits the arrow into his machine. "Here, Rupert," he calls. "Fix this line to something firm. That clothes pole will serve." Rupert takes the coil of twine across to the clothes pole, looking for a good place to tie it. In the same moment Bingo turns to talk to Bill and his smock catches the firing knob. "Oh, no!" he cries as the bowstring slams free.

Bingo's warning cry comes an instant too late. Rupert, reaching for the clothes pole, doesn't see what's happened and he is still clutching the coiled line as the arrow is fired. Before he knows what's going on he is yanked off his feet. Bill and Bingo stand frozen in horror. By the time they can catch their breath to shout "Let go!" Rupert is far too high to do that. All he can think is, "This can't be happening to me! Oh, that Bingo and his silly machine!"

RUPERT SEES DANGER AHEAD

Frightened to give a downward glance,
He hangs on tight and trusts to chance.

He's sure he'll crash, beyond a doubt.
But no! The arrow levels out.

Propelled by some unusual power,
It veers to the Professor's tower.

"The arrow's his!" Rupert decides.
Then dead ahead a huge bird glides.

Up, up streaks the arrow with Rupert clinging desperately to the coil of twine. He daren't look down and all the time through his mind go the words "What goes up must come down – and, oh, that's me!" That moment must come soon. But no! Instead of plunging back to earth the arrow levels out. After a moment Rupert risks opening his eyes. The arrow is flying level, but faster than ever! And above the rush of air he hears the arrow buzzing loudly again.

As the buzzing restarts the arrow changes direction, heading across Nutwood village towards . . . what? Then rupert sees what – the tower home of the Professor. Of course! Since it's his arrow he must somehow be controlling it. And, yes! There he is! On the roof. "He'll get me out of this," Rupert hopes desperately. But at that very moment a huge bird flies right into the path of the arrow. "Get out of the way, stupid thing!" Rupert yells.

RUPERT IS CARRIED AWAY

The two must hit! They must collide
Unless the creature moves aside

The bird – a courier for its King –
Snatches the arrow and its string

Then, catching Rupert round the waist,
It bears him off in angry haste.

"Come back!" the old Professor pleads
But on its way the great bird speeds.

Nothing, it seems, can stop the arrow hitting the bird. Rupert's shouted warning has no effect. He sees the Professor shouting too. Then in an instant the great creature seems almost to brake in mid-air and the arrow passes harmlessly in front of it. In the next instant the bird has swooped and snatched the arrow in its beak. Braked like that, Rupert starts to tumble, but even as he does he recognises the bird!

It is the Courier, the messenger, of the King of the Birds. He doesn't fall far. The Courier drops and catches him. To his surprise – when he can think again – he finds the bird's grip surprisingly gentle. That's all very well, but what's the creature going to do with him? On the roof of the tower he can see the Professor calling and beckoning to the bird to land. But the huge thing ignores the old man and carries Rupert away from Nutwood.

11

RUPERT REACHES A PALACE

As he looks down now Rupert sees
Peaks and lakes and scattered trees.

At last they near the journey's end,
Home of the Bird King – Rupert's friend

The mighty bird comes to a halt
And drops poor Rupert with a jolt.

The creature's still upset, it seems,
And fills the air with angry screams.

Soon Nutwood is left far behind. The land below becomes wilder yet to Rupert it is somehow familiar. Then he remembers. Of course! It's on the way from Nutwood to the Kingdom of the Birds! And that makes Rupert feel better, for more than once his adventures have led him to that strange place. He has even met the Bird King and been able to help him, so he feels sure the King will understand that he meant no harm to the Courier bird and send him home.

Now the palace of the King of the Birds appears through the clouds. The Courier glides towards one of its many terraces, hovers just above it and lets go of Rupert so that he lands with a nasty bump. Then it lands beside him, drops the arrow from its beak and lets loose a series of ear-splitting angry screams. Poor Rupert has to cover his ears. Plainly the huge creature is still very upset about its near miss with the arrow.

RUPERT IS LOCKED UP

In answer to its raucous shout,
A courtier and guards rush out.

"Dangerous flying is the charge,
This bear cannot be left at large!"

Rupert is marched across the yard,
On either side there stalks a guard.

"Now lock him in here while I fetch
The Chamberlain to judge the wretch!"

In answer to the Courier's screams two of the palace guards appear with a very pompous-looking bird courtier at their heels. At once the Courier starts to squawk what clearly is a complaint. As it listens the courtier looks more and more serious and when at last the Courier finishes it addresses Rupert: "You *are* in trouble! Dangerous flying, but even worse, interfering with a Courier on the King's business." Then it snaps an order at the guards who prod Rupert to his feet and start to march him away. "You've got this wrong!" he protests. "Be quiet!" snaps the courtier. "The Courier does not tell lies!" The little party halts at last beside a large birdcage which one of the guards unlocks. "In you go and wait while I fetch the King's Chamberlain," the courtier orders Rupert. "As the King's chief minister he is the one who must decide what is to be done with you."

13

RUPERT IS TOLD HE MUST WAIT

And then without another word,
Off struts this very pompous bird.

"The King alone can hear this trial
He won't be back for quite a while."

So Rupert's carried off to wait,
Perhaps for weeks, to learn his fate.

Just then a curious plane draws near.
His friend the old Professor's here!

The arrow is put into the cage with Rupert, the cage is padlocked and off struts the courtier to fetch the Chamberlain. When the two return they look stern, but the Chamberlain's first words cheer Rupert up: "Your offence is so grave only the King may deal with you." And, of course, that's what Rupert wants, believing that the King will understand he meant no harm. But the Chamberlain goes on, "However, the King is away on a trip and may not be back for weeks."

"You can't mean to keep me here until he comes back!" Rupert wails. "My Mummy and Daddy don't know where I am!" But all that happens is that the courtier orders the guards to bring the birdcage and follow it. So, slung on a pole, Rupert's birdcage prison is carried to a terrace on top of a high tower. Just as they arrive Rupert hears the drone of an engine. He looks up, and there is the strange little aircraft of his friend the Professor!

Rupert and the Boomerarrow

RUPERT'S FRIEND TURNS UP

Although he doesn't mean them harm,
The birds all scatter in alarm.

"No planes allowed!" they crossly squawk,
"Please!" says the old man, "Let me talk."

He tells them he's come specially
To ask them to set Rupert free.

"He's not to blame for that near miss,
For I controlled his flight with this."

Rupert is overjoyed at the sight of the Professor's aircraft. But he's the only one on that high terrace who is. The birds' open-beaked astonishment at its sudden appearance gives way to panic and they scatter as it lands. Then fear is replaced by anger when the engine stops and the Professor climbs out smiling. Hopping up and down with rage, the courtier squawks, "No planes allowed! How dare you bring that thing here of all places!"

"Please let me explain!" pleads the Professor. "I know you must dislike flying machines in your lovely kingdom but it's the only way I could get here to explain that Rupert is in no way to blame for the accident that almost happened to your, er, colleague. You see, I was testing my boomer-arrow and somehow Rupert got caught up by it." He goes to the aircraft and takes from it a strange device. "I was, in fact, controlling the boomer-arrow's flight with this."

RUPERT'S FRIEND HAS TO GO

"My boomerarrow's something new,
An arrow that comes back to you."

The Chamberlain won't change his mind,
Rupert, he says, must stay behind.

Reluctantly the old man goes,
He'll get no further here, he knows.

He calls to Rupert, "Hold on tight!
Don't worry, it will be all right."

The birds don't look at all impressed, but the Professor presses on: "I call my invention the boomerarrow because I can make it return like a boomerang – with this." Once more he indicates the device he is holding. "It got stuck somewhere while I was testing it – " Rupert nods. But the Professor is not allowed to go on. "Enough!" the Chamberlain cries. "I do not understand a word you say! The plain fact is this bear was flying with a dangerous arrow which almost put paid to the King's Courier and he must await the King's judgement. Now leave at once!" The birds look so fierce that the Professor backs towards his machine and climbs in. Rupert's heart sinks. But before the old man starts his engine he calls to Rupert, "Don't worry. It will be all right. But stay alert." Then he starts the engine and the aircraft rises. But above the noise Rupert is sure he hears him yell, "Hold on tight!"

RUPERT HEARS A SOUND

But as the aircraft disappears,
Rupert is very close to tears.

"The King dislikes all aeroplanes.
He'll be so cross!" a bird exclaims.

Imprisoned on a windswept tower,
Rupert grows glummer by the hour.

Then suddenly he pricks his ears,
What is that strange new sound he hears?

Dismally Rupert watches the Professor's aircraft disappear. He's so upset that he doesn't think about what his old friend said before leaving. He can only think about having to stay cooped up in this cage until the King of the Birds returns. Nor is he any happier hearing the Chamberlain say as the birds leave him, "The King will be so cross about the bear's friend bringing his aeroplane here. He dislikes the noisy things intensely."

Rupert can't remember ever having felt so miserable, caged, alone on a windswept tower. At least his parents will learn from the Professor where he is. Then he recalls the old man's parting words. "Stay alert." Not much chance of doing anything else in this wind. But what did he mean? And why did he shout, "Hold on tight"? Just then, above the whine of the wind, Rupert hears another sound – from something very close at hand.

RUPERT'S CAGE IS TOWED AWAY

A buzzing noise, there's no mistake,
The boomerarrow starts to shake.

The cage begins to rock apace
Until it topples into space.

The birdcage plunges through thick cloud
The buzzing now is really loud.

Out from the cloud he comes to find
He's left the birds' realm far behind.

In fact the new noise is coming from the boomerarrow. It has started to buzz again. Now the buzzing grows and the boomerarrow shakes as if trying to break free. The cage lurches towards the edge of the tower. Rupert grabs at the boomerarrow's tail meaning to untie the line and let it away. But in that second two things happen: He sees what the Professor meant by telling him to "stay alert" and "hold on tight" – and the cage topples into space!

For an awful moment Rupert is sure that the cage is plunging out of control. Then he realises that it is really being towed by the boomerarrow through the clouds on which the Bird King's palace stands. Above the swish of the air he hears the boomerarrow buzzing louder than ever. Suddenly they break out into brilliant sunshine and Rupert sees how far above the earth they are – and that they are still diving!

18

RUPERT IS RESCUED

The arrow levels, then it streaks
Towards the distant goal it seeks.

Straight to the guiding plane it flies
But takes the pilot by surprise.

The old Professor keeps his nerve
And causes Rupert's cage to swerve.

The cage and arrow come in reach,
He quickly catches hold of each.

Down sweeps the birdcage behind the speeding boomerarrow. Rupert just hopes that Bingo's twine is good strong stuff. Then the boomerarrow levels out and streaks towards a distant dot in the blue, a dot that grows until Rupert can see that it is the Professor's aircraft. His old friend must be controlling the boomerarrow from it. Now Rupert can see him clearly. His back is to the boomerarrow. Busy with the control device, does he know it is almost upon him? He turns.

His eyes widen in alarm. Can he get his machine out of the path of the boomerarrow in time? No! But he *can* change the boomerarrow's direction. He flicks a lever on the control device and boomerarrow and birdcage swerve at the last second. Then they make a wide circle, slowing until they stop beside the aircraft. The old man beams at Rupert as if nothing has happened. "I do hope you remembered to hold tight," he says.

"We don't want to upset the King.
We'll write and explain everything."

A welcome sight comes into view,
Bill, Bingo and his parents too.

Released at last, he leaves the cage.
It seems that he's been gone an age.

Happy now Rupert's home and free,
Everyone troops in for tea.

With Rupert and cage safely aboard, the Professor's aircraft heads for Nutwood. On the way the friends agree that they'll write to the King of the Birds to apologise for almost hitting his Courier and upsetting his courtiers. "He knows me," Rupert says. "I'm quite sure he'll understand." At last the Professor's home appears and waiting there are Mr. and Mrs. Bear, Bingo, Bill and the Professor's servant who was sent to fetch them.

With a hacksaw the Professor's servant frees Rupert in no time at all. Rupert's parents, of course, are overjoyed to have him back safely. As they all make their way indoors, Bingo and the Professor ask how they can make up for their part in Rupert's misadventure. "Well, first, a promise – no more bow and arrow experiments," laughs Rupert. "Done!" cry the others. "Then tea and muffins, lots of them," Rupert adds. "I'm starving!" The End

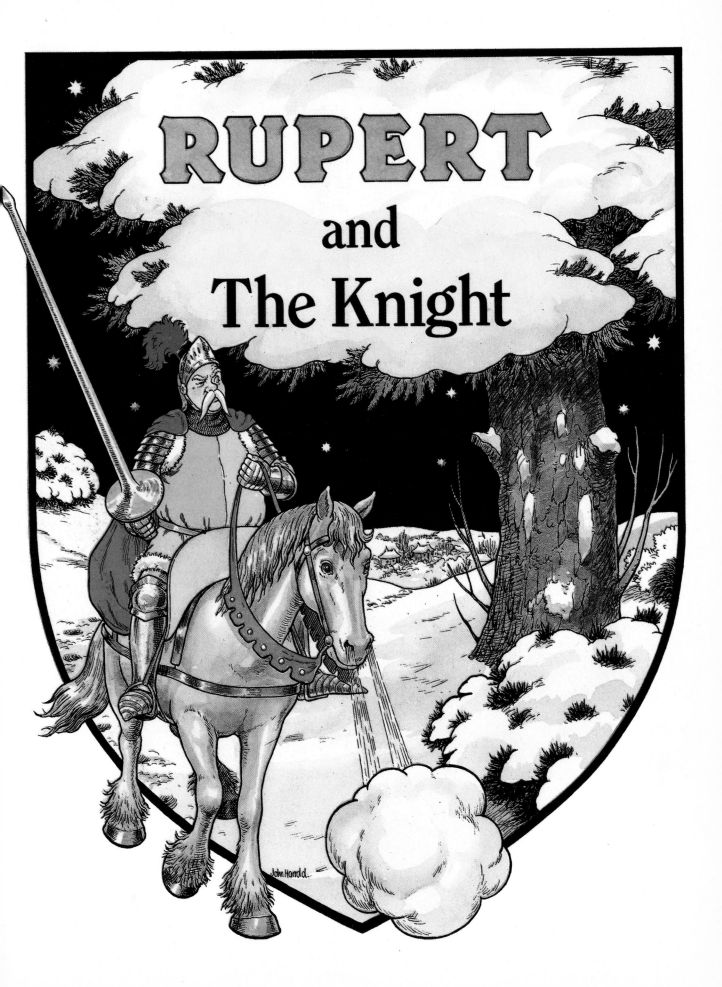

RUPERT HEARS SOMETHING ODD

"I can't recall such snow and ice,
So wrap up warmly's my advice."

Rupert heads for Bill Badger's house
But on the way meets Willie Mouse.

For Christmas Willie's had a boat
Which he is keen to see afloat.

Although it's cold as cold can be,
He knows a pond that's still ice-free.

For days and days, ever since Christmas, Nutwood has been gripped by ice and snow. Mrs. Bear looks at the thick frost on the windows and tells Rupert who is getting ready to go out in search of his chums to wrap up warmly and keep moving while he's out of doors. The snow crunches under his feet as he makes his way to Bill Badger's house. Then he spots another chum, Willie Mouse. "Hey, where are you off to, Willie?" he calls.

Willie, as it turns out, is off to sail the model boat he got at Christmas. "Sail it?" echoes Rupert. "With everything frozen solid?" "Not everything," Willie says. "I know a pond that's not frozen." "Oh, come on, Willie!" Rupert scoffs. "I can't believe that. Even the river's frozen!" Willie just smiles and moves off. But Rupert's curiosity is roused, for Willie seems so sure. "Hey, wait for me!" he calls and hurries after his small pal.

RUPERT'S PAL FALLS IN

Rupert doubts such a pond exists.
But Willie's seen it, he insists.

When Tiddler's Pool comes into view,
It's clear that Willie's tale is true.

Off Willie runs but fails to see
The roots of a snow-covered tree.

"Hey, look out, Willie!" Rupert calls,
Too late! He trips and in he falls!

"I didn't mean that I don't believe *you*," Rupert tells Willie when he catches up with him. "But it's jolly hard to believe that any outside water isn't frozen." Again Willie just smiles and presses on. "This leads to Tiddler's Pool," Rupert says after a bit. "Surely that's frozen!" "Not earlier today, it wasn't," Willie tells him. And a minute later he says, "There you are!" Rupert goggles. For below them Tiddler's Pool stirs in the slight wind.

"B-but how . . .?" Rupert stammers. Willie neither knows nor cares. He's too intent on trying out his new boat. He scampers down to the pool. But he is so excited he doesn't notice a snow-covered tree root across his path. Rupert does and shouts a warning. Too late! Willie's toe catches in the root. The boat flies from his grasp and next moment, before Rupert's horrified gaze, the little mouse plunges headfirst into the pool with an almighty splash.

RUPERT SAVES WILLIE

"Oh, help!" cries Willie in dismay
And Rupert acts without delay.

He wades to where poor Willie lies.
The water's warm – to his surprise!

Now Willies's safe, but even so,
He's soaking wet from head to toe.

In wet clothes he might catch a chill;
They must get home before he's ill.

Rupert doesn't hesitate. Tearing off his coat he dashes down to the pool where Willie is floundering and squeaking with dismay. Rupert braces himself for an icy shock as he wades into the water. And a shock is what he gets. For, far from being icy, the water is almost tepid! Rupert has known Tiddler's Pool colder on a hot summer day. Luckily the water's not deep and he is able to wade out to Willie, get him to his feet and help him to the bank.

Rupert is soaked up to the waist but poor Willie is sopping wet all over. After the mysterious warmth of Tiddler's Pool the cold is all the more biting and Rupert is worried for his pal. "Come on, we must get you home before you get a chill," he urges. Already the little mouse is beginning to shiver. Rupert wraps his coat around Willie's shoulders, picks up his boat and starts for home. As he goes he keeps wondering about that warm water.

RUPERT MEETS A KNIGHT

It's so cold Willie starts to freeze.
Shouts Rupert, "Someone help us please!"

Just then a horse comes into sight.
It's ridden by an ancient knight.

He lifts his visor and enquires
What kind of help Rupert requires.

The friends are soon wrapped in his cape.
They've really had a close escape.

Soon, however, Rupert has more than the mystery of Tiddler's Pool to trouble him, for, despite Rupert's coat, Willie is shivering so badly he can scarcely stumble along. Finally he slumps to the ground and can't be budged. "Oh, do get up!" pleads Rupert. "I can't carry you and I won't risk leaving you and going for help." But Willie's too cold to care. All Rupert can think of is to shout for help. Almost at once there is the thud of hooves and through the trees comes the strangest sight – a knight in armour. He raises his visor and speaks: "You crave succour?" "I-I don't know," stammers Rupert. "But we do need help." "Same thing," says the knight. "Sometimes forget folk today don't always understand knightly talk. Well, can I help?" When he's been told what's happened he lifts the pals onto the horse, wraps his cloak round them and asks, "Whither?" "Whither?" repeats Rupert. "Oh, I see – my cottage, please."

RUPERT HEARS HIS TALE

To Rupert's home they quickly ride
To where it's warm and dry inside.

Sir Claud then tells the Bears his tale:
He's following a dragon's trail.

They've had an awful job to get
Him not to challenge Pong-Ping's pet.

Rupert still feels the ancient knight
Thinks Pong-Ping's pet's the one to fight.

By the time they reach Rupert's home he has learnt that the knight is Sir Claud and is able to introduce him to his parents before pouring out his tale. Indoors, while Rupert and Willie are dried, Sir Claud explains his presence in Nutwood. He has trailed a dragon he's been after for ages to here. He's never actually *seen* this dragon – only been told of it. But he's certain it *is* here. When Willie says that the only dragon in Nutwood is the one belonging to their Pekinese pal Pong-Ping, Sir Claud shouts, "Then that *has* to be it!" and wants to be off after it at once. The others have to argue hard to stop him, telling him repeatedly that it is just a pet and can't be his one. He seems to accept this and rides off to seek lodgings in the village. But at bedtime – Willie is staying while his clothes dry – Rupert says, "I can't help feeling that Sir Claud still thinks Pong-Ping's dragon is the one he's after."

RUPERT GOES SLEDGING

Next morning Willie's right as rain
And Rupert sees him home again.

"Hi!" Algy calls. "Let's have a run
In my new sledge! It's really fun!"

The two pals drag it up a hill
And meet Sir Claud, who's searching still.

He tells them he's convinced his foe
Is Pong-Ping's pet. The pals cry "No!"

Next morning Rupert takes Willie back to his own house, none the worse for his ducking. In fact, Willie is already beginning to think of it and the rescue by Sir Claud as rather an adventure. As the two part Rupert wonders if he should go and warn Pong-Ping about Sir Claud and how he's had to be talked out of going after Pong-Ping's pet dragon. But then he hears his name called, and there's Algy Pug. "Come and have a run on my new sledge!" he cries.

That sort of invitation can't be resisted so Rupert joins his chum and they head for the high common. Rupert has just told Algy about the dragon-hunting Sir Claud when who should appear but the knight himself. He has been searching for hours, he says, without a trace of a dragon. "Yet I am certain it is here," he insists. "You know, I'm sure Pong-Ping's dragon must be the one I hunt!" "No! No!" chorus the pals. "It's only a little pet!"

RUPERT HAS A CLOSE ESCAPE

Down a steep hill the two pals race
At really far too fast a pace.

They hit a bump! They leave the snow
And flying through the air they go!

"Hold tight!" yells Algy as they soar.
A crash must surely be in store!

What follows gives the friends a shock,
They've found a cavern in the rock.

As Sir Claud rides off muttering doubtfully to himself, Rupert wonders aloud if he should go and tell Pong-Ping. But he's so looking forward to trying out the new sledge that he's ready to agree when Algy says they might only worry Pong-Ping needlessly and, anyway, Sir Claud seems pretty harmless. So the pair of them find a slope and are soon hurtling down it very fast . . . too fast! For when the sledge hits a bump it takes off like an aircraft.

In an instant the tingling fun of racing downhill turns to dismay. "Hold tight!" yells Algy. Rupert doesn't have to be told. He's hanging on as hard as he can. Ahead looms the glittering face of another steep slope, and it looks terrifyingly hard. But it isn't! Instead of smashing into a solid hillside the sledge slices through a sheet of frozen snow which has been concealing the entrance to a steep and rocky cavern.

RUPERT DISCOVERS A DRAGON

It's just like something in a dream.
A dragon stands beside a stream!

The two pals see, here underground,
The old knight's dragon they have found.

"Sir Claud!" the dragon cries with fear,
"Oh please don't tell him that I'm here!"

Into the stream it puffs great flames,
"You thawed the pool!", Rupert exclaims.

The sledge careers down a steep slope with our pair desperately hanging on. At last a bump jolts them clear just as they reach the bottom. Luckily neither is hurt. The cavern they're in is a big one with a stream running through it. But they are not alone. Sharing it with them is a dragon, not especially large and not at all fierce. In fact, it looks rather alarmed. And it looks twice as alarmed when Rupert cries, "This must be the dragon Sir Claud's after!"

"Oh, don't tell Sir Claud I'm here!" pleads the dragon. "I've never harmed a soul. Yet he hunts me just because knights of old were *supposed* to. He's never even met me." And with that it breathes a gust of flame into the stream. "Excuse me," it says. "Dragons have to breathe flame every so often. Down here the safest way's into the water." "*That's* why Tiddler's Pool was warm!" cries Rupert. "This stream must flow into it and you're warming it!"

RUPERT IS ALARMED

The dragon wails and begs our pair
Not to reveal its secret lair.

They meet Sir Claud who's now quite sure
It's Pong-Ping's pet he's looking for.

Cries Rupert, "Algy, off you go.
Tell PC Growler all you know!"

Now, Rupert has a plan in mind,
But first the dragon he must find.

Rupert can't wait to tell everyone why the pool wasn't frozen, and says so. "Oh, promise you won't!" pleads the dragon. "Sir Claud will get to know I'm here!" So, of course, the pals promise and it's a very relieved dragon they leave when they go. But they haven't gone far when they are hailed by Sir Claud: "Still can find no trace of the dragon! Yet I *know* it's here. So I've decided Pong-Ping's just has to be it, and I'm off now to challenge it!"

"He can't mean it!" gasps Algy as Sir Claud rides off. "He does!" says Rupert. "He's very single minded." "More like *simple-minded*," Algy cries. "We must do something!" "Then run and fetch Constable Growler to Pong-Ping's house as quickly as you can," Rupert says. "Tell him what's happening. I'm going back to the dragon." So the pals abandon the sledge and hurry away. A few minutes later Rupert is running up to the hole the sledge made in the hillside.

RUPERT GETS HELP

*Down to the cavern he descends
To tell it what Sir Claud intends.*

*The dragon listens, then agrees
To come and help the Pekinese.*

*The pair arrive at Pong-Ping's gate,
Just hoping that they're not too late.*

*Sir Claud adopts a fighting stance,
Bellows his challenge, points his lance.*

The dragon is rather alarmed to see Rupert back. "Don't tell me Sir Claud's on his way!" it quavers. "No, but he's on his way somewhere else," pants Rupert and pours out the story of how Sir Claud has convinced himself that Pong-Ping's pet is the dragon he's after. "And you can't tell him because of your promise to me," the dragon says after a pause. It swallows hard. "Right, where's Pong-Ping's house?" it sighs. "Lead the way!" "Thanks!" Rupert says quietly.

As they hurry to Pong-Ping's house the dragon says, "I hoped it would never come to this – having to face Sir Claud. I'm not at all brave." "Yes, you are," pants Rupert. "Or you'd have held me to my promise and stayed hidden." The two reach Pong-Ping's house to find the very startled Peke and his pet peering out at Sir Claud who has levelled his lance at the door and is bellowing, "Dragon, I, Sir Claud, challenge you to mortal combat!"

RUPERT STOPS A FIGHT

"Wait! Here's your dragon!" Rupert cries.
Sir Claud swings round with popping eyes.

But will they fight? Before that's clear
Algy and Growler both appear.

"To hunt a dragon or to fight
Without a licence is not right!"

Then PC Growler, looking grim,
Says that the knight must come with him.

"Wait! Here's your dragon!" At Rupert's cry Sir Claud swings round and his eyes pop. The dragon nods. Silence. "Well –" Sir Claud and the dragon begin. "After you," the dragon offers. "Well, I suppose we'd best get on with the, er, combat," mumbles Sir Claud. "Must you?" Rupert asks. Sir Claud stares. "It's my job to slay this dragon!" he says. "If you do you won't have a job," argues Rupert. "Hadn't thought of that," admits Sir Claud. Just then Algy and PC Growler arrive.

"Please dismount and let me see your dragon-hunting licence!" demands Growler. Sir Claud's jaw drops. "I need no licence!" he cries, climbing down. "In Nutwood you do!" says Growler. "And since plainly you don't have one I'll have to take you in while we sort this out." "How long will that take?" demands the knight. "Couple of days," Growler reckons. And Rupert notices that, far from being upset, Sir Claud seems glad not to have to fight.

RUPERT SAYS GOODBYE

It's plain the dragon cannot stay,
So Growler sends it on its way.

Sir Claud seems sad to see it go
Just as they've met and said hello.

And by the time he's free, it's clear,
The dragon will be far from here.

It's odd, thinks Rupert, how things end:
He's sure Sir Claud has found a friend.

Before he leads Sir Claud off, Growler turns to the dragon. "I'll trouble you," he says, "to be well away from here by this evening. I am not going to have dragons all over the place. Can't think what things are coming to. Pong-Ping's dragon's enough for us." "Why, yes!" the dragon agrees. "I'll be off at once." As Sir Claud is led away he turns and waves. "I hope I'll be seeing you, dragon," he calls. "He said that almost fondly," muses Rupert.

Rupert and his chums see the dragon off. "I'll be well away by the time Sir Claud's free," it says. "Hope I've not been too much trouble." Then off go Rupert and Algy for the sledge. As they make their way home Rupert reflects, "D'you know, I think Sir Claud would be unhappy without the dragon to pursue. And the dragon would miss him. I just know Sir Claud wouldn't – even if he could – have slain the dragon and even if Growler hadn't turned up when he did!" The End.

RUPERT

*Says Rupert, "Though I do like snow
I shan't be sad to see this go."*

It has been so cold for so long in Nutwood that even Rupert who likes snow has had quite enough of it. "My snowman's been here so long it's quite like an old friend," he jokes to Mrs. Bear as he goes in for tea. But later that evening as he's getting ready for bed Mrs. Bear says, "I do believe it's a bit warmer." She opens the window and cries, "Look! The icicles are beginning to melt at last!"

and the Thaw

That very night it seems at last
The days of snow and ice are past.

Next day the snow has almost cleared.
His snowman's all but disappeared!

Next day the snow has all but disappeared and Rupert's snowman is a pile of watery snow topped by a hat and scarf. As it happens today is a half-holiday and it is lunchtime as Rupert and Bill Badger head for home. Bill is just saying that his snowman, too, had melted into a shapeless heap by this morning, when from behind a tree the pair are passing a voice hisses, "Hey, Rupert!"

Bill's saying, "Mine did just the same,"
When someone calls out Rupert's name.

*It's Jack Frost and he's as upset
As either pal has seen him yet.*

*"The snow," he cries, "was meant to stay.
I've missed your snowmen by a day!"*

*"The Weather Clerk's to blame, and so
We'll have to see him. Come, let's go!"*

*Off Rupert goes to back up Jack.
To tell his folk Bill hurries back.*

"Jack Frost!" Rupert gasps as from behind the tree steps someone he's met several times, the son of the Winter Monarch, King Frost. "What are you doing here? We've just had a thaw!" "Yes, and you've had it a day too soon!" cries Jack. "Each year the Clerk of the Weather and I agree the date of the thaw so that I can collect snowmen and take them to serve my father. But the Clerk has sent the thaw a day early. My father will be far from pleased!"

"But what's that to do with us?" Rupert asks. "I want you to come with me to see the Clerk of the Weather," Jack replies. "You see he always suspects that my sister Jenny and I are playing tricks on him, and it's true we have sometimes. I need you to back me up about the thaw. We can be back in no time." "Go on!" Bill urges. "I'll tell your parents where you've gone." So Rupert agrees, gives Bill his satchel and sets off with Jack for the highest spot around.

RUPERT FLIES ON THE WIND

Jack finds a high spot where they stand.
He whistles and takes Rupert's hand.

A mighty wind sweeps up the pair
And soon they're flying through the air.

Higher and faster, on they fly
Until they reach the clear blue sky.

Soon they should see how matters stand,
For here is where the weather's planned.

Having travelled with Jack before, Rupert knows what to expect. When they reach the highest spot on Nutwood Common they scramble onto a big rock. "Hang on tight. Remember?" Jack says and takes Rupert's hand. Then he produces a little pipe which Rupert recognises – the whistle which summons wind to take Jack wherever he wants to go. He blows it and at once a great wind bursts upon the pair and sweeps them high into the air. Then faster than any bird – very much faster – Rupert and Jack are carried through the wintry sky. The land below becomes a blur then disappears as they soar into the clear blue, and head for the Clerk of the Weather's strange headquarters in the clouds. Rupert has met the Clerk before and knows him for a fussy old soul and one who plainly won't take kindly to being teased even by King Frost's children. But now – just ahead – the towers of his place appear among the clouds.

RUPERT MEETS THE APPRENTICE

To call the Clerk Jack has to shout.
He doesn't seem to be about.

"The Weather Clerk's on holiday
And I'm in charge while he's away.

Jack tells him what they've come about.
The youth seems not at all put out.

On this month's last day, as I should,
I sent the thaw to your Nutwood."

The wind slackens and Rupert and Jack glide down to land gently on a wide terrace. There's no sign of the Clerk himself so Jack hails him: "Weather Clerk, are you there? It's Jack Frost and Rupert Bear from Nutwood is with me!" "Oh, hello!" comes a voice from behind them and they turn to see a young man. "The Clerk's off on holiday for a few days, leaving me in charge. I'm his apprentice. I'm learning the weather business, if you see what I mean."

"You're actually in charge of the weather?" Jack sounds as if he can't believe his ears. "My master must have a break some time," the apprentice says. "Anyway, I'm quite able to look after things." "Then why send a thaw to Nutwood too soon?" snaps Jack. "Too soon?" echoes the other. "Never! There's what the Clerk agreed with you." He points to a notice: "Nutwood thaw, end of January." He grins smugly: "And today's the thirtieth – the end of January!"

RUPERT SPOTS WHAT'S WRONG

He's sure the month has thirty days.
"No, it has one more!" Rupert says.

"Oh dear!" he wails. "You are quite right,
The snow should stay until tonight."

"I have an idea!" Rupert cries.
"You'll have to send us fresh supplies."

"With extra snow we'll build once more
The snowmen melted by your thaw."

"The thirtieth isn't the end of January!" Rupert protests. "Yes, it is," the apprentice says and starts to recite, "Thirty days hath September, January –" "January!" squeak the others in disbelief. "Look!" cries Rupert and he lifts today's page on the calendar pad to reveal "JAN 31". "That silly rhyme!" wails the youth. "I always get it wrong!" "Even if you'd got it right you should have left the thaw 'til night!" Jack snaps. "Wait, I've an idea," says Rupert. "You," he tells the apprentice, "must find us a good supply of snow for Nutwood at once. My pals and I will build our snowmen again and Jack can collect them for King Frost. "But I can't tamper with the weather," the apprentice bleats. "You already have," says Jack. "Here's your chance to make good your mistake." The youth looks stricken and moans, "Oh, dear!" But he does start turning wheels, twiddling knobs and spinning dials.

RUPERT FOLLOWS A SNOWCLOUD

The prentice works the snow controls
And into sight a huge cloud rolls.

"Now let's get going straight away,"
Says Jack. "There's no time for delay."

So back to Nutwood our two speed,
Together with the snow they need.

As the cloud stops Jack Frost cries, "Good!
It must be falling in Nutwood."

Soon the apprentice points out of a window to where a huge cloud has appeared. "That snow was meant for Tibet," he says. "But when I pull this lever it will go at top speed to Nutwood. Get ready to go with it. I'll give you a signal when I'm set." So Rupert and Jack go out onto the terrace, now surrounded by seething cloud. Jack produces his whistle and tells Rupert to hold tight. Rupert watches the apprentice. The youth raises his hand. "Now!" Rupert cries. Jack blows his whistle and as he and Rupert are swept into the air the great snow cloud begins to move. It's so huge it scarcely seems to be moving but, in fact, it's as much as Jack and Rupert can do to keep up with it. At last it slows and stops. "Good!" cries Jack. "We must be over Nutwood. It'll be snowing down there. Now, we're going to have to dive through the cloud so hold very tight, Rupert. Now down we go!" And the pair plunge into the grey mass.

RUPERT RETURNS TO NUTWOOD

To see what's happening below
They plunge through thickly swirling snow.

As from the cloud the two break clear,
Rupert can see his pals quite near.

Jack says,"I hope you will agree
To build more snowmen just for me."

They'll be back soon, the chums declare
With gloves and scarves and coats to wear.

"Keep your eyes peeled!" Jack shouts. "We're bound to be pretty close to the ground when we come out of the cloud." So Rupert forces himself to keep his eyes open, although for what seems a long time there is nothing to see but a grey and white swirling mass. Then suddenly he can see a familiar landscape, already snow-covered. "Look, Jack!" he cries. "Look there! Bill, Algy and Willie Mouse!" And next moment Jack and he are swooping towards his excited pals.

Bill Badger has already told the others about Rupert's mission with Jack to the Weather Clerk. So all Jack has to tell them is why the thaw came too soon and to ask them to build their snowmen again for him. Although they have until next day Jack urges them to get the job done straight away – just in case of any more slip-ups. So off go the three to get the other chums and collect the things they'll need. "Fetch my coat, please, Bill!" Rupert calls.

RUPERT'S PALS BUILD SNOWMEN

At Jack's suggestion they decide
To build the snowmen side by side.

In pairs they pile and roll the snow
And soon the snowmen start to grow.

Each team does everything it can
To build the very best snowman.

"King Frost has ruled, you ought to know,
No one may see the snowmen go."

By the time Rupert's chums start arriving the snow has stopped falling and the ground has a thick carpet of white. Jack greets them: "It's very kind of you to help me by agreeing to build your snowmen again. But this time let's have them all in one place so that I shan't have to round them up from all over Nutwood." So the chums split up into their building pairs and in no time at all the snowmen are beginning to take shape again with each team trying to outdo the others. It is getting dark as they put the last touches to their creations. Jack signals to Rupert that he'd like a word with him. "This is embarrassing," he whispers. "Your chums have been very helpful but they mustn't see me fly off with the snowmen. No one's supposed to. It's King Frost's rule. Yet I hate to seem rude and ungrateful." "Don't worry, Jack," Rupert smiles. "I'll explain when you've gone. They're a good bunch. They'll understand."

42

"Good work!" cries Jack. "And I can tell.
They'll please King Frost, my father, well."

Now Jack Frost asks the pals if they
Will for a moment turn way.

A fierce cold wind begins to blow
As Jack Frost and the snowmen go.

The pals hear as they turn again,
Jack Frost call, "Rupert will explain!"

When the snowmen are complete Jack gathers the pals about him. "You've done a grand job," he says. "My father King Frost so looks forward to having the snowmen at court. He'd have been terribly upset not to have them. So as well as my thanks I give you his." Rupert and the others grin happily. Jack goes on: "I've one more favour to ask of you. Will all of you please turn your backs for a moment?" Obligingly all of them turn away from Jack and the snowmen. Only Rupert among them knows what is going to happen. There is a sudden shrill whistle and at once the pals find themselves facing into a wind so strong they have to shut their eyes. A faint voice calls, "Rupert will explain!" Everyone swings round. Jack and the snowmen have gone from where they were standing a moment earlier. Everyone looks up. They are just in time to see Jack and the snowmen disappearing into the sky which is now quite dark.

RUPERT EXPLAINS EVERYTHING

"Now what was Jack Frost playing at
To leave behind our backs like that?"

"It's King Frost's rule," comes the reply,
"No one should see the snowmen fly."

At home his parents wait to know
The facts about this latest snow.

It starts to thaw again that night,
But Jack's well clear so that's all right.

For a moment there is silence then everyone starts talking. "Well! . . . I must say! . . . He might at least . . ." Then they turn on Rupert. "What did he mean 'Rupert will explain'?" Podgy demands. So, as he promised Jack, Rupert tells them about King Frost's ruling that no one should see Jack fly off with the snowmen and how embarrassed Jack was at having to leave like that after they'd all been so kind and how he was really very grateful. "That's all right then!" they all laugh.

The adventure over, Rupert and the others troop back to their homes, happy to have been able to help Jack Frost but vowing they've had enough of snowmen for a long time. Rupert's parents can hardly wait to hear all about his trip and the apprentice's silly bungle. At bedtime Mr. Bear looks out at the snow. "I do believe that youth has started the thaw already!" he says. "Then it's as well Jack decided to get the job done at once!" Rupert laughs. The End.

44

These two pictures of Rupert and Algy in Bingo's workshop look identical, but there are fourteen differences between them. Can you spot them? (*Answers on Page 99*)

Rupert's Parachute Game

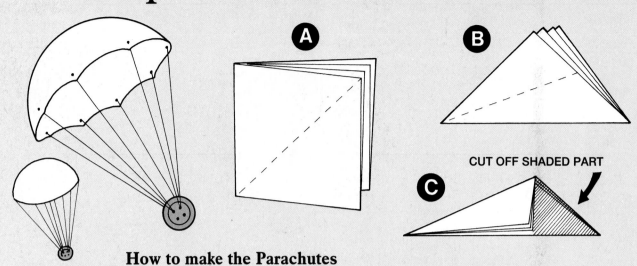

CUT OFF SHADED PART

How to make the Parachutes

Use pieces of tissue paper eight inches square, (203mm) one for each player. Fold the paper in half and in half again as in (A), again as in (B) and finally as in (C). Cut off the spare part shown shaded, and you will have an eight-sided parachute shape as in (D). Make a pin-hole near each of the eight points shown. Next prepare the block of coloured numbers for your game. Make a hole in each dot of the numbered squares, then cut some lengths of cotton, eight pieces nine inches (230mm) long for each player, and some smaller pieces not more than two or three inches (50/75mm) long. Thread the pieces of cotton through the numbered holes, putting one in each and mixing them well. Pull the cottons through so that only an inch (25mm) of each cotton shows, the rest being hidden under the page.

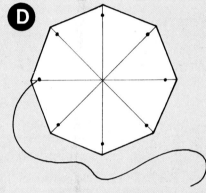

THREAD A COTTON
THROUGH EACH HOLE

2	4	1	5	2	6	3	1
5	1	2	3	5	2	1	5
4	1	3	1	1	5	1	6
3	2	4	5	2	5	3	2
6	3	5	2	3	1	4	3
5	1	2	5	6	4	2	1
1	2	4	3	1	6	2	4
4	3	6	1	4	2	3	5

How to play the Game

At each throw of the dice the player may choose any square which contains the same number as his score. He then pulls out the cotton. If it is a long one he keeps it for his parachute. If the cotton is a short one, it is not used. Sooner or later one player will win by being the first to collect eight long threads for his 'chute. He puts a cotton into each hole of his tissue paper, fastening it with a knot. The other ends of the cottons are tied to a button. Meanwhile, the other players go on with the game until each has enough long cottons to make a parachute. Hold the 'chute above your head and let it go, and it will open out and sail to the ground.

(MAXIMUM FOUR PLAYERS)

RUPERT
and the
Power Flower

RUPERT SEES A STRANGE DOVE

One fine warm day Rupert agrees
To go and fetch some groceries.

A sudden screeching in the sky
Makes Rupert stop and look up high.

"Look out!" cries Rupert, for above
A fierce hawk dives upon a dove.

The dove turns round and strikes the hawk
Which flies off with a frightened squawk.

It is a warm, sunny morning and Rupert is on his way to the village store in Nutwood to collect his Mummy's shopping. Because the weather is so fine he decides to take the long way round across the common. Suddenly scree-ee-eech! A shrill noise from overhead makes Rupert stop in his tracks and look up. He sees high above him in the sky a fierce hawk swooping on a dove, which seems to be carrying something in its beak.

"Look out!" cries Rupert as the hawk dives at the dove, its sharp talons at the ready. It looks as if nothing can save the poor dove, but at Rupert's cry it turns around and sees the sudden danger. To Rupert's amazement the peaceful-looking dove swings round and attacks the hawk. There is a great flurry of beating wings and feathers fly as the two birds fight, but in the end the hawk flies off screeching in fear with the astonishing dove in hot pursuit.

48

RUPERT FINDS A FLOWER

Triumphantly the dove's cries ring
But from its beak it drops something.

Rupert's very surprised to find
It's left some sort of flower behind.

He's just about to sniff it when
The dove comes winging back again.

"Hello!" cries Rupert but the bird
Now flies away at his first word.

"I can't believe it!" gasps Rupert. "Who ever heard of a hawk being chased by a dove?" Just then the dove gives a cry of triumph and the thing in its beak falls to the ground. Leaving his shopping trolley for a moment, Rupert runs forward to find a flower lying on the grass. He picks it up and finds that, although it looks pretty and delicate, its stem and leaves feel tough and strong. "How strange!" he thinks. "I wonder if it has a very strong scent?"

Before he can sniff the flower, though, Rupert hears a fluttering of wings and looks up to find that the dove has come back again. As it flies towards him he waves and holds up the flower to show the bird that he has found it. At this the dove flaps its wings in alarm, turns, and flies away high over the treetops. "I wonder why it has suddenly become so timid?" thinks Rupert. "I was only going to offer to return its flower."

49

RUPERT FEELS NO FEAR

*He smells the flower and feels as if
He's been made stronger by that sniff.*

*Then Rupert suddenly can hear
Thundering hoofbeats drawing near.*

*He turns to see a wild-eyed steed,
A cart-horse, bolting at full speed.*

*He doesn't cringe or cower. Instead
He leaps to grab the horse's head.*

Alone again, Rupert takes a deep sniff and finds that the flower's scent is as odd and unexpected as its curious leaves and stem. It isn't a sweet or very powerful smell but almost at once it begins to make him feel bold and fearless – as if there isn't a thing in the world that he can't do. A sudden thundering of hooves jolts him back to his senses. The ground trembles and he sees a swirling cloud of dust racing along the road towards him.

As it draws nearer, Rupert sees that it is a farm cart pulled by a runaway horse which is completely out of control. The driver has lost hold of the reins and it seems certain that there's going to be a very nasty accident. Without a moment's hesitation Rupert darts to the side of the road and gets ready to catch the horse as it gallops wildly by. As it draws level he leaps with outstretched arms, launching himself at the horse's head.

RUPERT STOPS A RUNAWAY HORSE

He grips the bridle and holds tight.
The horse resists with all its might!

Eventually it slows and stops
And safely to the ground he drops.

Cries Rupert, "Don't tell anyone,
Oh, please, about what I've just done!"

"How odd," he thinks, "I felt no fear
When I first saw that horse appear.

Rupert manages to grab hold of the horse's bridle and swings on it with all his might, trying to force its head down. For a moment it resists then its head drops, it slows and at last comes to a complete halt. Down Rupert hops and then hands the reins back to the grateful carter. "Why, bless me!" he declares. "Who would have thought that a little bear like you could stop this great big horse! If I hadn't have seen it with me own eyes I'd never have believed it!"

The old man is still muttering in amazement as he goes on his way and it is only then that Rupert thinks how alarmed his Mummy will be if she hears what he has been up to. "I say, please don't tell anyone what's happened!" he calls after the carter, but he doesn't seem to hear. Rupert sighs, picks up the strange flower he has dropped in all the excitement and continues on towards the village. "How odd," he thinks, "I wasn't at all frightened when I saw that horse bolting!"

While waiting in the village store
Rupert sniffs at the flower once more.

It's now that Rupert comes to find
He's left his shopping cart behind.

So calmly he just lifts the weight
And hurries home before he's late.

How Mr. Bear gasps with surprise!
He simply can't believe his eyes.

When he arrives at the village shop Rupert hands his list to the shopkeeper and waits while he makes up the order. He sniffs the flower once more as he stands there. At last a huge bag of shopping is ready to be loaded into his trolley. But where is it? In all the commotion he has left it behind on the common where he saw the dove drop the strange flower. "Oh dear!" the shopkeeper says, "this bag is far too heavy for you to carry…" But that doesn't seem to bother Rupert.

Taking it from the astonished shopkeeper, he simply hoists it on to his shoulder and marches out of the shop. People in the street stop and marvel at Rupert's astounding display of strength. And no one is more amazed than Mr. Bear, who is out in the garden when his son comes strolling up the path carrying not only the heavy shopping, but also the trolley which he has collected from the common on the way home.

RUPERT SURPRISES HIS PARENTS

His Daddy tries to take the sack
But soon is glad to hand it back!

And in the kitchen Mrs. Bear
Is speechless. She can only stare.

Then Mr. Bear demands to know
What's happened to make Rupert so.

He starts, "I think what made me strong – "
Then PC Growler comes along.

"Good gracious!" cries Mr. Bear, dropping his garden fork with a clatter. "Here, let me have that bag before you hurt yourself!" He takes the shopping in both arms – and at once almost collapses under the weight. "Perhaps I had better carry it indoors!" chuckles Rupert, as his father tries to stagger towards the house. He takes it from him with ease and goes into the kitchen. Mrs. Bear can't believe what she sees. How *can* Rupert be carrying such an enormous load?

Mrs. Bear sinks into a chair while her husband follows Rupert into the kitchen. How on earth can he possibly have managed to carry such a load all the way from the village shop, Mr. Bear wants to know. Perching himself on the table, Rupert begins, "I think it has something to do with..." He is going to tell them about the flower dropped by the dove. But at that moment striding up the garden path comes a familiar figure. "It's PC Growler!" cries Rupert.

"If everything I hear is true,
I'd like to have a word with you!"

He tells how Rupert saved the day
By stopping a wild runaway.

It's now that Rupert tells them all
About the flower the dove let fall.

His mother sniffs it thoughtfully,
"I wonder what this flower can be?"

I want a word with you, Rupert!" Constable Growler begins. "Oh, dear!" Rupert's Mummy exclaims, "whatever is the matter?" "There's no need for alarm," Growler replies, "But I've been told that Rupert has been a bit of a hero!" And he goes on to tell the astonished couple how Rupert stopped the runaway horse and doubtless prevented a very nasty accident. "But how can Rupert have stopped a horse?" gasps Mr. Bear, "and why has he suddenly become so strong?"

"It's all to do with this flower, I'm sure!" Rupert says, and tells them about the dove with the flower in its beak driving off the fierce hawk. "I don't know what it does exactly," he says. "But it's something very special!" "Well, it certainly looks very pretty," says Mrs. Bear. And she picks up the flower to take a closer look. Before Rupert can stop her she holds it close to her nose, shuts her eyes and takes a deep sniff...

RUPERT GETS A MESSAGE

She lifts the heavy bag with ease.
Growler's amazed by what he sees!

Growler decides the flower can't stay
But must be safely locked away.

Out playing later, Rupert's told
He's wanted by his friend of old.

He leaves at once but does not know
The brothers Fox have seen him go.

"H'm, not much of a scent," she murmurs and asks Constable Growler if he would like to stay and have a cup of tea. "Tea, yes…that would be…very nice," the policeman stammers, for his eyes are popping out of his head at the way Mrs. Bear lifts the heavy bag of shopping with one hand! "It's that flower!" he gulps. "I will have to take it to the police station with me for safe-keeping. Who knows what might happen if it falls into the wrong hands?"

Later that day Rupert is playing on the common when someone calls his name. He turns to find the servant of his friend the Professor. "My master would like to see you at once," whispers the little man. 'It's about something we believe you found. Please come." "Right," Rupert says and off the pair go. But they've been seen by that mischievous pair, the brothers Ferdy and Freddy Fox. "That looks interesting," Ferdy says. "Let's follow them. Come on!"

*The old Professor says that he
Has flowers that Rupert ought to see.*

*Their super-pollen makes you strong.
It's an experiment gone wrong!"*

*"I want to get rid of the lot.
Let's fetch the one that Growler's got."*

*Each word of this the foxes hear,
Then scuttle off with an idea!*

"Did you find a strange flower today?" Rupert gasps at the Professor's first question when he finds him in his garden. "H–how – ?" he begins. "I heard about your feats of strength," smiles his old friend. "And I put two and two together. Come, I'll show you." In a greenhouse he shows Rupert bunches of flowers like the one he found. "An experiment gone wrong," he says. "I bred a super-pollen so that bees would make more honey. But it made the flowers tough and the bees as strong as eagles. So I gathered up all the flowers to get rid of them but a dove flew down and stole one!" "So that's it!" Rupert cries and pours out the story of how he found the flower and what has happened to it. "Then let's go and collect it from PC Growler," the Professor cries. "I'll fetch my jacket." All of this the Fox brothers have overheard and, unseen, off they race back to Nutwood. And they are sniggering as they go.

RUPERT'S FLOWER DISAPPEARS

*Laughing, away the Foxes race
As our lot get to Growler's place.*

*"The flower has gone!" Growler declares.
"The foxes told me it was theirs!"*

*Outside a bus is revving hard
But can't advance a single yard.*

*The uproar is the foxes' fault;
They've brought the huge bus to a halt!*

As Rupert arrives at the police station with the Professor and his servant he spies Ferdy and Freddy Fox running away down the street. They are laughing in a most unpleasant way. Next minute Rupert and the others learn why. They've got the flower "I thought you'd sent 'em for it, Professor," cries Growler. "They said it was yours and that they'd come to collect it!" "Oh, no!" groans Rupert. "They must know what that flower can do..."

His words are drowned by a sudden din outside. People are shouting and the local bus is roaring away as if it's engine is about to burst. "I don't believe this is happening!" gasps Growler as they run out of the police station. No matter how hard the driver tries, the bus cannot move an inch because the foxes are holding on to its back bumper. "Stop that, you rascals!" shouts Growler. They let go and as the bus lurches forward, Freddy and Ferdy laugh louder than ever.

57

"Stop that!" yells Growler, "Do you hear?"
But neither shows the slightest fear.

They lift the poor man in the air,
Then hook him up and leave him there!

Now off they dash to have some fun,
Just look at all the things they've done...

A postbox balanced on a wall
As if it weighed nothing at all.

PC Growler bounds after the Fox brothers, promising them a lesson they won't forget. But as the furious policeman is about to pounce one of them sniffs the stolen flower and effortlessly swings him right off the ground. Next moment he finds himself dangling from the railings by his belt. "You'll be sorry for this!" he yells. "Just you wait!" But the brothers have no intention of waiting and they dash off leaving poor Growler wriggling helplessly.

"After them!" cries the Professor who up to that moment has been too thunderstruck to act. Now with Rupert and his servant he sets off in pursuit of the unpleasant pair. Although, with their start, they are soon out of sight, it isn't difficult to tell where they have been. Mischievous at the best of times, when armed with the Professor's super-pollen flower, they can go in for super-mischief. As, for instance upending a letter box on top of a wall!

RUPERT MEETS A TINKER

The tinker's donkey in his cart,
Another trick the twins thought smart!

"They went that way, the wretched pair!
I think you'll find they're over there."

A signpost lies torn from the ground,
A clue to where they might be found?

"The windmill's stopped!" Rupert exclaims,
"More of the foxes' fun and games!"

"We must get the flower before that pair do something truly awful!" declares the Professor when they see the next of the pair's pranks – a tinker's donkey lifted into it's own cart, much to the fury of the unfortunate tinker, who is left with the problem of how to get it out! "They went that way!" he tells the Professor. "I saw them run off as I came back to my cart, though how they managed to lift up my poor donkey I shall never know!"

They follow the tinker's directions and after a while come across a signpost which reads "To Windmill". It has been torn out of the ground and tossed carelessly to one side of the road. "Which way now?" asks the Professor. Then Rupert notices something and points to the windmill itself. "The sails have just stopped turning, even though there's a fair wind blowing. I'm sure the mill is where we'll find Ferdy and Freddy!"

59

RUPERT FINDS THE FOXES

There, by the mill, the brothers stand.
Freddy has stopped it with one hand!

Then suddenly he looks surprised,
It's harder than he realized!

The wind begins to turn the sails,
And Freddy's swept up! How he wails!

His brother lets the flower drop
And runs to try the sails to stop.

When he and the others reach the windmill Rupert sees that his guess was right. There stands Freddy, holding the sails still with one hand, while his brother, who has the flower, keeps the miller trapped inside. "Stop all this and give me the flower at once!" the Professor booms, but Ferdy's only answer is a mocking laugh. His brother seems much quieter and Rupert thinks that he looks rather worried. "Freddy's having trouble keeping that sail still!" he murmurs.

"The wind's too strong!" whimpers Freddy, "I can't hold on for much longer..." The next minute he is swept off his feet by a sudden gust and the sails of the windmill begin to turn once more. "Hold on tight!" yells his brother as Freddy is lifted high into the air. "I'll soon get you down!" He darts forward to seize the next sail but in his haste loses his grip on the flower which falls to the ground just as the sail arrives.

RUPERT IS SWEPT OFF HIS FEET

He too is swept up off the ground
And now both foxes spin around

Then Rupert sees the flower he's dropped,
Perhaps the sails can still be stopped?

The old Professor calls out, "Wait!"
But Rupert hears his cry too late.

He grabs the sail. He's swept up too.
It seems now that the flower won't do.

Ferdy jumps up and catches hold of the sail as it spins by. To his dismay he finds it is too powerful for him to stop. No matter how hard he pulls he can't prevent it turning, and next instant he is carried high into the air just like his brother. "They must have forgotten to sniff the flower." thinks Rupert, "That's why they can't hold the sails still." He picks up the flower from where it landed when Ferdy dropped it and takes a long, deep sniff.

"No, don't!" shouts the Professor when he sees what Rupert has in mind, but it's too late. Rupert has already launched himself into the air and caught hold of a sail as it begins to travel upwards. To his astonishment the flower seems to have had no effect on him at all. It takes every ounce of his strength just to stop himself from falling. There is certainly no question of his stopping the windmill and helping Ferdy and Freddy to safety.

RUPERT NEEDS HELP

Up with the sail poor Rupert flies,
"Hold on!" the old Professor cries.

"I'll get you down, but for the task
I'll need the contents of this flask."

He pours a splash on to the flower,
Then deeply sniffs to gain more power.

He grips a sail. He finds that he
Can stop the windmill easily.

Now there are three small frightened creatures clinging desperately to the great sails of the windmill. If nothing can stop it from turning, how are they ever going to get down again? As Rupert dangles high above the ground he looks down and sees that the Professor has picked up the flower. He seems to be pouring something into it from a small phial he has taken from his jacket pocket. "Hang on!" he calls up to the three. "I'll get you down."

Having poured the contents of the phial into the flower, the Professor swirls it round and takes a deep sniff. Then he reaches out with one hand and, instead of being swept off his feet like the others, he calmly brings the sails to a halt. "You are quite safe now," the Professor calls up to Rupert and the foxes. "I'm going to stop each sail in turn and get you down one at a time. Remember to hang on tightly as we go round!"

RUPERT IS SAVED

The instant they're safe on the ground
The brothers Fox are homeward bound.

Released, the miller rushes out,
Not knowing what it's all about.

"This super-pollen's caused such fuss.
Get rid of it! It's dangerous."

As Rupert later homeward strolls
He sees Bill fishing for tadpoles.

The sail with Freddy on it comes slowly past and at last the shivering fox is lifted to safety. The Professor does the same for Ferdy and then Rupert. "Why couldn't I stop the sails?" he asks. "Because the flower's pollen was all used up," his friend explains. "It doesn't last for ever. I had to give it some more of the super-pollen before it would work again." As he speaks the bewildered miller appears, just in time to see the foxes scuttling away.

The Professor decides that the Fox brothers have had enough of a lesson for one day. But their mischief has convinced him that the sooner the super-pollen and it's flowers are got rid of, the better. He asks Rupert to help him bury the flowers in a hole at the bottom of the garden while his servant gets rid of the last of the super-pollen. It's some time later before Rupert sets off for home. On the way he sees Bill Badger fishing for tadpoles.

RUPERT AND BILL ARE PUZZLED

His friend is suddenly upset
By something pulling at his net

Headfirst he tumbles with a shout,
And Rupert runs to get him out.

Something has pulled Bill, that is plain,
But what it was he can't explain.

"It seemed quite small," he says, "and yet
It's torn a hole right through my net!"

Rupert is about to call out to Bill when something extraordinary happens. One moment Bill is standing peacefully by the side of the pond, and the next, without any warning, he leaps in the air and plunges into the water! "What happened?" Rupert asks as his friend sits there gasping. "I've no idea!" splutters Bill. "I've never known anything like it. Something must have swum into my net and jerked me clean off my feet by giving it such a tug! At least that's what it felt like.

Although how something that big and as strong as that can be living in this little pond I just don't know." "Nor do I," says Rupert. "We catch tadpoles here every year but I've never seen anything else swimming about in it." He pulls Bill out on to dry land and they look at the net to see what he has caught. To their surprise it is quite empty. Something has torn a hole through the bottom and escaped. But what?

RUPERT GETS THE ANSWER

Then up the little servant comes.
"What's going on?" demand the chums.

"Oh dear!" he groans, "The fault is mine.
I should have left this warning sign."

"I tipped the pollen in this lake
And fed the tadpoles by mistake!"

Bill says that they're too much for him:
He's come out fishing – not to swim!

As Bill and Rupert stand talking together by the edge of the pond, who should come along but the Professor's servant. He is carrying a newly painted signpost and seems surprised to find anyone fishing there. Rupert tells him what has happened to Bill and asks if he has any idea what kind of creature can have torn a hole in his friend's net. "Oh dear!" says the servant, "I'm afraid I do. It's all my fault really, that's why I'm carrying this sign. It's that super-pollen!" he explains. "I'm afraid I foolishly dumped it in the pond without thinking and the tadpoles which live here have suddenly become as strong as can be." He shows them the sign which reads: "BEWARE DANGEROUS TADPOLES! NO FISHING UNTIL FURTHER NOTICE." "So that's what I caught!" laughs Bill. "Fancy being pulled in by a tadpole! It's too much for me I'm afraid. After all I've come here to go fishing, not swimming!" The End.

RUPERT and

From Nutwood one day three pals hike,
To see the Wise Old Goat they like.

It's just the weather for walking and Rupert, Willie Mouse and Algy Pug make the Wise Old Goat's hilltop home their goal. Their clever, rather mysterious old friend comes out to greet them and insists they stay for lunch. Then he ushers them into his cluttered workroom where he makes his experiments. From the start Algy is much taken with one of the machines. It is like a grandfather clock in a glass cabinet.

Algy's Misadventure

*He welcomes to his strange old house
Rupert, Algy and Willie Mouse.*

*Algy's enthralled for he's just seen
The History Clock time machine.*

"I say, Rupert, is that the machine that takes you back and forward in time?" he asks. "Yes, that's the History Clock," says Rupert who more than once has been whisked back to historical times by it. Of course, Algy wants to know how it works and, of course, Rupert who should know better than to fiddle with machines, has to show him. "Fetch me a stool to stand on," he says, "and I'll show you."

*With Rupert acting as his guide
He means to have a look inside.*

RUPERT EXPLAINS THE CLOCK

*"You set the hands up here to show
The year to which you want to go."*

*A long-past year shows on the face
When Algy steps inside the case.*

*Then Willie slips, he starts to fall
And grabs a large switch on the wall.*

*Down comes the switch. Contact is made!
At once poor Algy starts to fade.*

Perched on the stool, Rupert explains: "The numbers on the History Clock's face represent not hours but years. You set the hands for the one you want." He sets them at the year 1400. "Then you stand in the cabinet and shut the door." "Oh, let me!" pleads Algy. So Rupert removes the stool and lets him. Now Willie climbs onto the stool to examine the clock's face. He spots a switch near his head. "Does this work it?" he asks. "Careful!" Rupert cries.

Being timid, Willie feels that when he's told to be careful there's some danger near that he needs to be careful about. This makes him nervous which makes him clumsy. "What . . .?" He starts, teeters on the stool, reaches out to stop himself falling and grabs the switch. "Get out of there, Algy!" Rupert yells as the History Clock begins to hum. Desperately Algy fumbles at the catch of the cabinet door. But already his shape is beginning to fade.

RUPERT'S PAL ALGY DISAPPEARS

The Goat returns. The scene's a fright,
With Algy almost out of sight.

He tells the pals, "I greatly fear
I cannot bring him back from here."

"Without a disc he's out of reach.
All travellers must wear one each."

There's only one thing to be done,
Rupert must go and take him one!

The Wise Old Goat returns to an awful scene. Willie is sprawled, whimpering, on the floor while Rupert lunges at the door of the cabinet in which the last shimmering outline of Algy is just visible. Before Rupert can open the door Algy has disappeared. To a background of Willie's weeping Rupert stammers out his story of what has happened. "It's terrible!" he ends up. "More terrible than you know," says the Goat. "You see, from here we can't bring him back!"

"Can't we do anything?" cries Rupert. For his answer the Goat goes to the switch to turn it off and at the same time lifts a disc suspended from a hook below it. "When you have travelled in time before, Rupert, you have had such a Return Medal which brings you back here when you choose," he says. "One must be taken to Algy. I shall prepare it. We can't send Willie and I must look after the Clock. Will you go?" Rupert nods. The medal is hung about his neck.

69

The Wise Old Goat starts to prepare
The medal Algy is to wear.

"To come back all you have to do
Is press the button when you're through."

The time has come to take his place
Inside the History Clock case.

Poor Willie Mouse is close to tears
As slowly Rupert disappears.

At once the Wise Old Goat sets about putting together a Return Medal for Rupert to take to Algy. To quieten Willie's sobbing, he tells him, "Now, you mustn't upset yourself. As soon as Algy gets this, no matter where he is, Rupert and he will be back with us. All he has to do is push the button on the medal." When it is ready he hands it to Rupert. "It's the same as your one," he says. "Keep it somewhere safe until you hand it over to Algy."

Although he has travelled through time before and knows that the Return Medal works, Rupert still has butterflies in his tummy as he steps into the History Clock cabinet. "Aren't you scared?" quavers Willie. Rupert who prefers to be honest, just smiles. "Ready?" asks the Goat. Rupert nods and tucks Algy's medal into his pocket. He stands in front of the Clock and shuts his eyes. The Goat switches on the power and gradually Rupert starts to fade.

With smiling face and tight-shut eyes,
Back through the ages Rupert flies.

Then suddenly he lands somewhere,
An ancient, cobbled village square.

A crowd of people hurry by.
They cheer and shout – he wonders why.

What can it be that makes them run?
He tries in vain to ask someone.

The Wise Old Goat's cry "Good luck!" and a startled wail from Willie are the last things Rupert hears before he is swept back through the centuries. It's a strange, curiously pleasant feeling. Then he is aware that this time trip is almost over. He feels more wakeful and he can hear sounds that grow louder. Then suddenly he has arrived. He is in what seems to be a village square full of poeple. And they are all running very excitedly in one direction.

Oddly, no one seems to notice the sudden arrival in their midst of a small bewildered bear. There's so much noise and so many people that Rupert wonders how he's ever going to find Algy. What's going on? Why is everyone running? And where to? One or two folk spare a glance for him, their eyes caught by his – for them – strange costume. Rupert tries to stop and question one or two of them. But they brush past, shouting, "Long live the duke!"

RUPERT FINDS OUT WHERE HE IS

At last a small boy stops to say,
"Duke Algernon's come back today!"

He points to Rupert's modern clothes:
"He's wearing garments just like those!"

The boy runs off but Rupert blinks:
Could Algernon be who he thinks?

"This place is Nutwood long ago!
That castle tower's a place I know."

At last Rupert gets a boy to stop and asks what's happening. "Why, it's our beloved young duke!" cries the boy. "He's back!" When Rupert still looks puzzled the boy says, "You must be a real stranger in Nutwood not to know that our young Duke Algernon vanished many days ago and was given up for good. Then a little while ago he turned up in the market place wearing such outlandish gear with loose leg coverings – like those." He points to Rupert's trousers.

The boy hurries after the crowd, leaving poor Rupert with his mind awhirl. Nutwood! His own village as it was hundreds of years ago! And its young duke has mysteriously returned wearing modern trousers. Rupert is beginning to suspect who young Duke Algernon will turn out to be. He follows the crowd. The only building he recognises is the church – until he reaches a castle he never knew Nutwood had. Its round tower is now the home of his friend the old Professor!

RUPERT IS TAKEN PRISONER

*He wriggles through the crowd to see
Who this "Duke Algernon" might be.*

*And Rupert sees when once he's near,
It's Algy Pug the people cheer!*

*A trumpet sounds and silence falls.
"Hi, Algy! It's me!" Rupert calls.*

*He tries to join him but the knight,
Sir Guy, has Rupert thrust from sight.*

All Rupert can see by the time he reaches the castle is a solid row of backs. But with a lot of squirming and repeating "excuse me" over and over, he gets to the front of the crowd. "Long live our Duke Algernon!" cry the people. And there, standing at the top of some stairs between two knights – a pleasant-looking fair- haired one and a villainous-looking one with a dark beard – is the person they are hailing. "Gosh!" breathes Rupert. "It *is* Algy!"

Then a trumpet peals and a herald cries, "Be silent for Sir Guy!" The bearded knight raises his hand. Silence. Rupert seizes his chance. "Algy!" he shouts. "It's me – Rupert!" Sir Guy snaps an order to a hard-looking man at his shoulder. The man rushes at Rupert, grabs him before anyone can move and bundles him to a small archway. The last thing Rupert sees before being thrust down dark stone stairs is Sir Guy preventing Algy from following.

RUPERT MEETS ALGY'S DOUBLE

Down, down the two go 'til at last
Into a dungeon Rupert's cast

But someone else is in that place –
The real Duke who has Algy's face.

"A captive! Me! You wonder why.
He kidnapped me, that false Sir Guy!"

The Duke then asks the little bear
Who he is and why he's there.

Rupert finds himself in a passage lit by flaming torches. His captor halts at a door with a grille in it, unbolts it, thrusts Rupert inside and slams the door on him. In a dark corner behind Rupert something stirs. Rupert holds his breath. A figure rises from a bed of straw and advances into the light from the grille. Rupert gasps. For though the figure wears an old-fashioned hooded robe, his face is Algy's! "B-but . . . who . . .?" Rupert quavers.

"I am Duke Algernon de Pugge!" comes the answer. "Prisoner in my own castle! Kidnapped and cast here by my false steward Sir Guy who would take over my dukedom. He has told my people I have disappeared and will rule in my place until they believe I shall never return and he take over altogether. But who be you and whence come you?" "Oh, dear," thinks Rupert. "How on earth am I ever going to get him to believe this?"

Rupert tells him of Algy's plight,
Not mentioning the pair's time-flight.

"Sir Guy can now control, I see,
Your friend the people think is me!"

"It may well be we look the same,
But with this mark I'll prove my claim."

To beat Sir Guy they must get free.
Says Rupert, "Leave all that to me!"

Rupert knows perfectly well that the Duke will never believe the History Clock so he tells him that his friend, plain Algy Pug but as it happens the Duke's double, has somehow found his way here and been taken for the Duke and that he, Rupert, has come to take him home but been thrust down here before he can reveal who he is. "Alas, 'tis better still for Sir Guy!" cries the Duke. "Now he has one the people believe is me – one he can control completely!"

While the Duke goes on about how he should have made the fair knight, Sir Hal, his steward instead of Sir Guy, Rupert thinks hard. "If we got free could you prove you're the Duke?" he breaks in. The Duke pushes back his sleeve to show a star-shaped mark. "Your friend may have my face but he does not have this!" Rupert reaches for his Return Medal. "Then," he says, "we're going to get free and give you the chance to prove who you are!"

RUPERT AND THE DUKE ESCAPE

He hands Duke Algernon a disc,
Assuring him there is no risk.

In less time than it takes to tell,
The pair have vanished from their cell.

The centuries go racing past
Until they reach today at last.

Laughs Rupert, "Yes, it's me who's here.
This isn't Algy, though, I fear."

"Get free?" repeats Duke Algernon. "But how? Do you have some magic means, eh?" Rupert, who is fishing from his pocket the Return Medal meant for Algy, says, "Not exactly, though you may think so. But trust me, do as I say and we shall be free in a flash." He hangs the medal about the Duke's neck and tells him, "When I say 'Go', press the button on this." The Duke looks unsure but nods. "Then – go!" Rupert cries. They both press – and begin to disappear.

Rupert knows what to expect when being whisked through time by the History Clock and has come to like the strange feeling of soaring over the centuries. As far as he can tell, the Duke is enjoying it too. Then quite suddenly they are back in the Wise Old Goat's workshop with the clever creature himself and Willie. "Rupert! Algy!" the pair gasp. "Well, it's certainly me," laughs Rupert. "But this is not Algy. And we want to go back again right away!"

76

RUPERT TELLS WHAT'S HAPPENED

"The only way to set him free
Was bring him back to now with me!"

The Duke cannot believe his ears
When Rupert's words he overhears.

The Wise Old Goat sees he's confused
And tells him how the clock is used.

"Before returning here, please do
Persuade the Duke to drink this brew."

Only Rupert is not bewildered. So while Duke Algernon gazes, wide-eyed and silent, at his surroundings, Rupert explains. "So we had to use the History Clock to get free which meant coming back to our time," he winds up. "Now we must return to the Duke's time to get Algy." The Duke has heard this with growing alarm. "Witchcraft!" he cries. "No, no!" the Goat reassures him. "But Rupert is right. Both of you must go back to your time, Duke, at once."

As simply as he can, the Goat tells the Duke about his History Clock. The Duke doesn't truly understand but at least he now believes he has travelled in time. As he takes his place for the return to his own time he says, "My people shall know I have seen the future!" Before Rupert joins him he is slipped a small flask by the Goat who whispers, "Before you and Algy leave get the Duke to drink this. It will save him from any ill effects of his time trip."

Now all is set, the clock's switched on,
The travellers will soon be gone.

In old Nutwood they reappear,
No one's about; the coast is clear.

Without a sound they slowly crawl
Through bushes to the castle wall.

The Duke unlocks a secret door.
Used by the dukes in days of yore.

As Rupert takes his place beside the Duke for the return trip, Willie who has been silent so far asks the Duke, "Aren't you frightened?" The Duke smiles. "Nay," he says. "'Tis pleasant, I find." The Wise Old Goat, hand on switch, asks, "Ready?" Rupert and the Duke nod. The Goat switches on the power. A moment later they are in Nutwood, 1400 AD. No one is about. "Happily for us, 'tis the evening meal time," the Duke says, pulling up his hood.

Now that they're back in Nutwood, the first task facing Rupert and the Duke is to get into the castle unobserved. They must surprise the wicked Sir Guy. So although it is the evening meal hour with everyone indoors, they take a secret route through bushes and trees, the Duke with his hood up in case they run into anyone. At last, hidden among deep bushes, they reach a low door. From a secret pocket the Duke produces a key.

Using an ancient passageway
The two press on without delay.

They reach a curtain which the Duke
Then pulls aside so they may look.

A banquet's being held, they see.
A scene of lavish revelry.

But then Sir Guy spots Rupert there.
He points and bellows, "Seize that bear!"

Beyond the door lies a narrow tunnel. The Duke whispers to Rupert, "My ancestors used this secret way when they went out disguised to mingle with the people and find out what they were really thinking." The passage ends in steps up to a stout door. The Duke signs to Rupert to wait below while he unlocks the door and listens. Then he beckons him to follow. Facing them, just inside the door, is a curtain. From the other side of it comes the sounds of revelry.

The Duke pulls aside the curtain to reveal the castle's banqueting hall full of warmth, light, music and laughter. There is only one miserable face – Algy's. He is seated in the place of honour between wicked Sir Guy and honest Sir Hal. Everyone is too busy eating, drinking and talking to pay any attention to the two figures by the curtain. Then Sir Guy looks up – straight at Rupert! He leaps to his feet and points at him. "Seize that bear!" he screams.

The guards close in. The Duke cries, "No!"
And bares his arm the star to show.

"By this mark you know who I am.
Sir Guy's deceived you with a sham!"

The wicked knight is led away.
Duke Algernon has won the day!

Now Rupert has one final task:
To give the duke the Wise Goat's flask.

A shocked silence falls on the hall. Two men-at-arms go to seize Rupert. Then the silence is shattered by a cry. "No!" It is Duke Algernon. He has thrown back his hood and is holding up his bare arm to show the star mark. "By this sign you know I am your true Duke!" he shouts. "I have been the secret prisoner of false Sir Guy. Arrest him and his henchman!" a great cheer goes up as the men-at-arms who were about to seize Rupert lay hands on the pair.

The hall is in uproar. Honest Sir Hal has Sir Guy and his henchman marched away to the dungeons. Algy, who hasn't at all understood what's going on, rushes to Rupert. "What . . . ?" he starts. "Tell you later!" grins Rupert before turning to the Duke and saying, "Please excuse us! We must get back." The Duke says it's a pity they can't stay and help him celebrate, but he agrees. Then Rupert remembers something and produces the flask the Wise Old Goat gave him.

RUPERT RESCUES ALGY

The Duke up-ends the flask and drinks.
"It's time to go now," Rupert thinks.

As they grow faint the pals can tell,
They're fading from his mind as well.

The homeward journey's very fast
Our two are soon back from the past.

The Goat greets Algy with a hug,
He's so relieved to see the pug!

So that his guests won't be upset by seeing Algy and Rupert disappear, Duke Algernon leads them to a quiet corner. There Rupert hands him the little flask, explaining that its contents will save him from any ill-effects of his time trip. While the Duke drains the flask Rupert hangs the Return Medal round Algy's neck. "Are you ready?" he says. A strange look comes over the Duke's face. "Who are you?" he begins. "Go!" Rupert cries. And Algy and he start to fade.

To Algy and Rupert it seems only a moment since they were in Nutwood of five centuries ago. Now here they are safely back in their own time. And here to greet them are Willie Mouse and the Wise Old Goat. Most of the time the Goat is extremely dignified but he's so overjoyed to see the pair safely back that he happily swings Algy off his feet. "Now, Rupert," Algy cries. "Tell us what all this has been about." And so, of course, Rupert does.

81

"That castle," Rupert asks his friend,
"What happened to it in the end?"

"It all burned down." The Goat explains,
"Except one tower, which still remains."

The three friends leave and vote to go
To see the only tower they know.

"The Old Professor lives there now,
Let's tell him where we've been, and how!"

When Rupert has told his story he says, "I wonder what happened to Duke Algernon." After consulting an old history book the Goat tells him: "The Duke lived happily to a great age. Sir Guy was banished and much later Nutwood Castle — but for the round tower — was burned down." Rupert has another question: What was in the flask he gave the Duke? Something to make him forget the time trip, he's told. "We couldn't have him remembering the future," the Goat says.

Adventure over. Rupert, Algy and Willie start back to Nutwood. The Wise Old Goat sees them off. "Come again soon!" he calls. "But next time don't fiddle with things!" The pals' way home takes them past their friend the Professor's tower, the only bit of Nutwood Castle left. "I vote we go and tell him we were in his house earlier today," Algy chuckles. "More like, five hundred years ago!" laughs Rupert. And the three pals press on home for tea. The End.

Rupert's Picture Puzzle

This picture was painted by Alex Cubie for Rupert's Adventure Series. It shows Rupert and his Mummy playing a game which you can join in too. Every letter in the alphabet is represented by at least one of the objects in this room. Can you write down what they all are? *(Answers on page 99)*

Rupert's Memory Test

Please don't try this memory test until you have read all the stories in the book. When you have read them, study the pictures below. Each is part of a bigger picture you will have seen in a story. When you have done that, see if you can answer the questions at the bottom of the page. Afterwards check the stories to discover if you were right.

CAN YOU REMEMBER . . .

1. Why is this bird cross?
2. What has this switch just done?
3. What is behind this door?
4. What is Growler asking for?
5. What is in this tube?
6. Which year is Rupert setting?
7. Why is Jack blowing his whistle?
8. Why does Bingo need this?
9. What happens to Willie next?
10. What *should* happen on this date?
11. What is towing Rupert?
12. Whose shoes are these?
13. What has Rupert just seen?
14. What have these reindeer eaten?
15. What has he forgotten?
16. Why is Bill in the water?

RUPERT
and
Rika's Return

John Harrold

RUPERT RECEIVES A LETTER

Rupert's pal Rika writes to say
With Santa's team she's on her way.

"She says she'd like to rest them here.
But where can we put six reindeer?"

Says Mr. Bear, "I know the thing!
The garden of your chum Pong-Ping!"

So Rupert hurries out to seek
His pal and quite soon finds the Peke.

If you've read the story Rupert and Rika you will know that Rika is the little Lapp girl to whom Santa Claus gave the job of looking after his reindeer on their summer holiday in Lapland. Rupert helped her to get the job. This story begins when Rupert gets a letter from Rika to say she is taking the reindeer to Santa for Christmas and will rest them in Nutwood. She's arriving next evening and asks Rupert to signal by lamp to show where her reindeer may land and spend the night without being seen by anyone. Of course, everyone is delighted. But where can they put the reindeer? The Bears' own garden's too small. Then Mr. Bear announces, "I know just the thing! Your Peke pal Pong-Ping's garden. It's large and very private!" So out rushes Rupert in search of Pong-Ping and with the greatest good luck meets him returning from a shopping expedition to Nutwood village stores.

RUPERT GETS PONG-PING'S HELP

To lodge the reindeer he agrees.
The need for secrecy he sees.

Eavesdropping from behind a tree,
The Foxes scent a mystery.

So they are lurking nearby when
Rupert and Pong-Ping meet again.

When they see what swoops from the skies
The Foxes can't believe their eyes.

Pong-Ping has heard Rupert speak of Rika but he can hardly believe what Rupert has to ask of him now. "Tomorrow night!" he cries. "Santa's reindeer! In my garden?" But of course, being a pal, he agrees and, what's more, sees that their presence must be a secret. He does, though, insist that they be tethered where they can't get at any of his rare plants. So it's all settled. What the pals don't know is that the Fox brothers have been spying on them.

Next night Rupert goes to Pong-Ping's garden where his chum is waiting. But so – in hiding – are Ferdy and Freddy Fox. Although they did not hear all that Rupert and Pong-Ping said they guess that something important is afoot and, being nosy as well as mischievous, they want to know what. "I say, what's Rupert up to?" Ferdy breathes as Rupert flashes his torch at the sky. Then their eyes pop as down swoops a girl on a reindeer followed by other reindeer.

RUPERT AND HIS PAL MEET RIKA

*"Rika, please leave your reindeer where
They can't eat any plants, they're rare."*

*The foxy pair have heard this too
And think what mischief they might do.*

*A pity, Rupert's parents say,
That Rika has so short a stay.*

*She feels the same: "Nutwood is quite
The nicest place I know – Goodnight!"*

The reindeer land. Rika springs to the ground. "Rupert!" she beams. "I'm so happy to see you again!" Smiling, Rupert introduces her to Pong-Ping who tells her he is honoured to have Santa's reindeer as guests. Then politely he asks if they might be tethered where they can't reach his rare plants and Rika tethers them where he suggests. Then she and Rupert thank Pong-Ping and start for Rupert's home. The Fox brothers have seen and heard it all!

Rupert's parents like Rika. "Such a shame you can't stay longer," Mrs. Bear says. "Oh, I shall be able to spend most of tomorrow here," Rika replies. "I shan't leave 'til after dark – Santa doesn't like the reindeer to be seen before Christmas." "Then I'll be able to show you some of Nutwood," Rupert says. Later, tucked up in the spare bedroom, Rika smiles and says, "Everyone here is so nice." Plainly she doesn't know the Fox brothers.

RUPERT AND RIKA GET A SHOCK

Next day, a scrabbling, and here is
Pong-Ping's pet dragon in a tizz.

It hurries off as if to say,
"My master wants you. Quick, this way!"

"They've been untied, and as you see,
Have eaten from that bush-like tree."

He hurries off to have a look
At his rare trees and bushes book.

After breakfast next day Rupert and Rika are getting ready to go out when there is a frantic scrabbling at the front door. Mrs. Bear opens it and there's Pong-Ping's pet dragon looking very upset. It is behaving in the oddest way, making as if to go then turning back, looking expectantly at Rupert. "I think Pong-Ping has sent it to fetch us," Rupert says. "Come on, Rika, let's follow it!" And off they scamper after the dragon towards Pong-Ping's house.

Rika gives a great wail of dismay at what greets them there. The reindeer are lying around a small bush-like tree. "Someone's untied them!" cries Pong-Ping. "And they've eaten leaves from the Dragon's Boon tree!" Vainly Rika tries to rouse them with the bell Santa gave her. "I'm going to get my book on rare bushes and trees," Pong-Ping announces and rushes indoors. "There must be something in it about Dragon's Boon leaves and what they do if you eat them."

89

RUPERT FINDS A CLUE

Rupert spies something, thinks, "Hello!
That's Ferdy Fox's scarf, I know."

"My lift to China we must take,"
The Peke says, "for the reindeer's sake."

"They've eaten Dragon's Boon, I'm sure.
And China's where we'll find the cure."

"This note is to the police to say,
'Keep watch on this while we're away.'"

While Pong-Ping is consulting his plants book and Rika is trying to rouse her reindeer, Rupert spots something caught on a branch. He recognises it. Just then Pong-Ping re-appears. "See what I've found!" Rupert greets him. "It's Ferdy Fox's scarf. He and Freddy must have let loose the reindeer." But all the excited Peke will say is, "We'll deal with them when we get back!" "From where?" Rupert demands. "From China!" cries Pong-Ping.

Pong-Ping opens the big book he's brought out. "The leaves the reindeer have eaten," he recites, "are used to cure toothache in dragons. They're far too strong for other creatures. They knock them out. Only the Ching leaf found in my part of China will rouse them. We must go there in my lift. There, the mandarin Li-Poo's Dragon Master may be able to help us." Then he turns to his pet and says, "Take this note to Constable Growler, the Nutwood bobby."

RUPERT GOES TO CHINA

"In this right through the earth we ride
To China on the other side."

The lift has not been used for weeks
And starts with many groans and creaks.

"Half-way we must do this I've found,
So we arrive the right way round."

Pong-Ping cries, "Hurry up, you two!
We must find my wise friend Li-Poo!"

Pong-Ping explains that the note to Growler is to ask him to keep an eye on the reindeer while he and the others are in China. Then, as he leads the way to the lift he explains how it goes through the earth to China, turning over half-way there so that you come out right way up. "I'm afraid it hasn't been used for weeks," he says, ushering the others into it. And, indeed, it takes several stabs at the starter button to get the thing moving.

After its jerky start Pong-Ping's lift seems to settle down. Then comes the half-way point where it must turn over. Pong-Ping presses the button to do this. The lift starts to turn . . . and sticks! Only a great deal of jabbing at the button gets it to complete the turn and continue its journey. The moment the lift's doors open at the journey's end Pong-Ping races out towards a fine house shouting, "Come on, that's Li-Poo's place!"

"Her reindeer team ate Dragon's Boon,
And they are due at Santa's soon."

"I'll call my Dragon Master who
Will fetch what's needed," says Li-Poo.

He's told, "There is no time to waste.
So bring the medicine with haste!"

The smoke from roasted leaves of Ching
Must be inhaled, translates Pong-Ping.

Rupert and the others find Li-Poo sunning himself on a terrace. Pong-Ping introduces his companions. In fact, Li-Poo has met Rupert before and remembers it, but the young lady? So Pong-Ping explains about Rika's reindeer eating the Dragon's Boon and now having to have Ching leaves to rouse them. At once Li-Poo rises, crosses to a gong and strikes it. "I am summoning my Dragon Master," he says. "He will know what to do."

A tall man answers Li-Poo's summons. Li-Poo addresses him in their own language. "He looks after Li-Poo's dragons," Pong-Ping whispers. "They're much respected hereabouts." The man bows and hurries away to return in no time at all with a small jar. He proffers it to Rika and speaks. Pong-Ping translates: "The Ching leaves in this pot must be roasted and your reindeer must be allowed to breathe in the smoke from them."

Li-Poo says, "Now's no time to stay
And be polite. Quick! On your way!"

"No!" cries the Peke. "What awful luck!
This wretched lift of mine is stuck!"

"I know who might repair the thing –
Li-Poo's smart grandson, young Ting-Ling."

But no! The pals learn with dismay,
The boy Ting-Ling has gone away.

Rupert and the others can hardly wait to get away. But they make no move for that would be disrespectful to Li-Poo. The old man smiles. "This is no time for fine manners," he says. "Off with you at once!" Our three gabble their thanks and make a dash for Pong-Ping's lift. "It's going to be all right!" Rika laughs. She speaks too soon. For when Pong-Ping tries to get the lift to start the wretched thing won't work no matter what he does.

"Can't you do anything to make it go?" Rika pleads. Pong-Ping shakes his head. "I'm no good with machinery," he confesses. "But wait! Li-Poo's grandson Ting-Ling – you know him, Rupert – he's good at mending things." So moments later Li-Poo is astonished to see his three young visitors re-appear. But his face falls when he hears their plea. "My grandson Ting-Ling," he groans, "is away on a visit and will not be back for many days."

93

RUPERT SUGGESTS A SOLUTION

*"Perhaps," says Rupert, "we three might
Return home on a dragon flight."*

*"The only dragon that would do,"
They're told, "cannot be spared for you."*

*But Li-Poo's moved by Rika's tears
And says, "You shall fly home, my dears!"*

*Says he, "The Dragon Laws or not,
I want the long-range dragon brought!"*

Things look black. Then Rupert speaks up: "You have dragons that fly, sir, and I know they can fly a long way. Mightn't we return home on such a dragon flight?" At once the Dragon Master is summoned and told what is wanted. He looks dismayed as he blurts out his answer. Pong-Ping translates: "Only the long-range dragon would do and that can't be spared. It must stay here to take Li-Poo to the Imperial Palace should the Emperor want him."

At this Rika bursts into tears. Everything seems to be against her. Li-Poo is dismayed. He tries to comfort Rika for a moment then he seems to make up his mind. He speaks to the Dragon Master and what he says startles Pong-Ping. Li-Poo addresses the Peke: "Yes, I *did* say that Emperor's Dragon Laws or not you three shall fly home!" With that he leads the way to the open ground below the terrace onto which the Dragon Master is leading a large dragon.

RUPERT GOES HOME BY DRAGON

The dragon knows which way to go.
"Good luck!" cries Li-Poo far below.

Soon our three, far above the ground,
By dragon flight are homeward bound.

Growler is waiting as they land,
A squirming Fox in each large hand.

"I caught this pair of rascals when
They came for Ferdy's scarf again."

Once Rupert and the others are securely on the dragon's back the Dragon Master speaks to it quietly. "He's telling it which of the ancient Dragon Ways is best for us," Pong-Ping explains. Before Rupert can speak, Rika asks Li-Poo, "Are you sure you won't get into trouble?" Li-Poo smiles: "The Emperor will agree that a guest in our country must come first. Good luck!" And in a moment the dragon is airborne and Nutwood bound.

On the way Rupert asks Pong-Ping what he meant about ancient Dragon Ways. "It's got something to do with dragons travelling through time as well as space," Pong-Ping says. "I've never really understood it." It's almost dark when they reach Nutwood but light enough to see in Pong-Ping's garden the Fox brothers in Constable Growler's grasp. And soon he is explaining how he caught them when they came sneaking back for Ferdy's scarf.

A little stove is brought and fired
To roast the Ching leaves as required.

They start to smoke, the time is near
To try to rouse the six reindeer.

A sleeping reindeer deeply breathes
The smoke that from the medicine wreathes.

"It works!" cries Rika in delight.
"That means that we can leave tonight!"

While Growler is talking to Rupert Pong-Ping hurries indoors and re-appears with a small stove and a tiny pan which has a lid with holes in it. "It's a herb-roaster," explains Pong-Ping. "It should do for the Ching leaves." Rupert opens the jar they have brought from China and fills the pan with the leaves from it. On to the stove it goes and soon it is giving off spicy fumes. "Right," Rupert says. "Let's see if it works."

Nervously Rika takes the smoking pan from the stove. Directed by Pong-Ping she holds it under a reindeer's nose. For a moment nothing happens. Then the animal gives a great sigh, its eyes snap open and it is fully awake. Rika gives a great cry of delight. "It works!" she laughs. "Oh, now we must rouse the others as quickly as we can. We can still get away tonight. We can still be at Santa's in time!"

RUPERT'S FRIEND IS SET TO GO

In turn the other reindeer take
A long deep sniff and they're awake.

"It's been away too long and so
Li-Poo's great dragon's had to go."

"I think you should let that pair go.
And Santa would agree I know."

"You let the reindeer eat from there,
So you shall dig it up, you pair!"

Now that one reindeer is awake it's only a matter of minutes 'til the rest are up and about. "For goodness sake," says Pong-Ping, "tie those creatures up so that they can't have another bite at the Dragon's Boon tree." While he's making sure that the reindeer are quite safe his pet dragon scampers up to tell him that Li-Poo's dragon has had to leave. "It'd been away too long," says the pet. "It simply had to get back."

At last Rika is ready to go. "Before you go, miss," Growler says to her. "What shall I do with this pair?" He thrusts forward the Fox brothers. "Let them go," Rika asks. "I know that's what Santa would prefer." So Growler releases them, but Pong-Ping still has something to say. "You're not getting off so easily," he tells the Foxes. "You let the reindeer eat that Dragon's Boon, so you'll come back here tomorrow and dig it up!"

RUPERT GETS A SURPRISE

Once it is dark goodbyes are said.
The reindeer leave, by Rika led.

"Dragons and reindeer! I don't know!"
Laughs Growler. "I had better go!"

"An extra present! Let me see!
Who is it from? What can it be?"

A badge! A note to say, "Thank you",
From Santa Claus and Rika too.

Night has fallen. The moon rises and it's time for Rika and her team to leave. Rupert, Pong-Ping and Growler watch her and the reindeer rise into the dark sky, waving 'til she's out of sight. The Fox brothers scuttle off. Then Pong-Ping says he must get his pet's supper and Growler says he'll walk home with Rupert. At Rupert's gate he stops and says with a wink: "I'd best get back to the police station. Reindeer, dragons, who knows what folk'll be reporting."

Christmas morning. Rupert is awake bright and early. Yes, all the presents he'd wished for are here. But wait! Here's an unexpected one. He tears it open. It's a glittering badge, a reindeer's head. And there's a note with it. "For special services to Christmas," it says. "Pong-Ping's got one too." It is signed "Santa Claus". But someone else has added a signature – "Rika". And what's more there are two kisses!   THE END.

Follow me each day in the **Daily Express**

ANSWERS TO PUZZLES

Spot the Difference: 1. Number of buttons Algy's waistcoat, 2. Number of cross-checks Rupert's trousers, 3. One not two pieces of wood under bench, 4. No handle on vice, 5. Hammer on floor turned round, 6. Bingo's glasses gone, 7. No badge Bingo's cap, 8. Central window bar gone, 9. No bracket under shelf, 10. One wheel gone from go-cart, 11. No turn-ups Algy's trousers, 12. Extra stick in can on bench, 13. No steering nut and bolt on go-cart, 14. End of rope on floor gone.

Rupert's Picture Puzzle: A – Arrows, B – Basin, C – Chair, D – Desk, E – Engine, F – Fan, G – Gun, H – Hat, I – Ink, J – Jug, K – Kettle, L – Lamp, M – Mirror, N – Net, O – Orange, P – Pan, Q – Quiver, R – Radio, S – Sword, T – Top, U – Umbrella, V – Vase, W – Watch, X – On building brick, Y – Yacht, Z – Zebra. See how many others you can find.

John Harrold.